The Children's Bedtime Book

NEW YORK

CONTENTS

**All stories retold by
MAE BROADLEY
Illustrations by
MARY SMITH, JO EAVES and ANNA DZIERŽEK**

Copyright © 1983 by World International Publishing Limited.
A Pentos Company. Great Ducie Street, Manchester, England.
First published in USA 1982
by Exeter Books
Distributed by Bookthrift
Exeter is a trademark of Simon & Schuster Inc.
Bookthrift is a registered trademark of Simon & Schuster Inc.
New York, New York.

ALL RIGHTS RESERVED

ISBN 0-671-05615-8

Printed in Czechoslovakia

SLEEPING BEAUTY

THIS is the story of a far-off kingdom and of people who lived and things that happened long, long ago.

Among the green valleys of Germany, nestling against the side of a steep hill, there was once a fairytale castle. With flags flying from its turrets and its many windows twinkling in the sun, the castle presented a smiling face to the world. Inside, too, there was music and laughter. For this was the home of a king and his wife, kind and just rulers who were well-loved by all the people of that kingdom.

Yet, in the midst of all this happiness, the queen would sometimes become quiet and her lovely face grow sad.

"For the joy of having a child I would change places with the poorest in the land," she confided one day to her lady-in-waiting as, through her window, she watched the peasant children outside at their carefree play.

The queen's longing was shared by the king. But the years passed and still no heir was born to that kingdom.

Now among the king's subjects were twelve wise women. Nobody knew from whence these women came, but many believed that they were old as time itself and everyone knew that they possessed the powers of magic. One of these women saw with pity the queen's growing sadness and, being a kindly little soul, she decided to grant the queen's wish.

So it came about that, one summer's day, a princess was born.

Such was the joy of the proud parents that they wanted to share their happiness with all their friends and subjects. The king ordered that a great feast should be prepared. Invitations were sent out, and cooks and housemaids and courtiers raced up and down the castle stairs and corridors in a frenzy of preparation.

It was a splendid occasion. All the richest and noblest families in the land attended, filling the great hall with colour and laughter. Present, too, were poor peasants, dressed in their best Sunday clothing, their well-scrubbed faces shining and red. All sat down at the same table and were served with the same food on the king's best gold plates.

From the head of the top table, the king looked round with pleased affection at those who joined with him in celebrating his daughter's birth. His gaze rested with special gratitude on the wise women, seated near him, who would shortly use their wonderful powers to ensure that the life of the young princess was blessed with every grace and good fortune.

One, two, three . . . without knowing why he did it, he counted them. Then an awful realisation came to him. There were only eleven wise women present. Somehow, in

issuing the invitations, he had omitted one of the twelve.

His face paled and his hand, holding a wine-glass, trembled. Then, seeing his dear wife looking at him in concern, he tried to dispel the cold fear that had suddenly gripped his heart.

He would apologise personally to the fairy woman, he told himself, and . . . yes! that was it, he would invite her to another celebration, which would be attended only by his most intimate friends. She would be flattered by this special treatment and would readily forgive the unintentional insult that had occasioned it.

Even as he made these plans the wise women rose from the banquet table. They walked, in single file, to the raised dais on which stood the cradle where the baby princess lay.

Up the three steps went the smallest of the women. More like a farmer's wife than a dainty fairy, she was round and rosy, and her voice, when she spoke, was high and nervous.

"My s-s-sister fairies and I w-wish to bless the ba-by princess at w-w-whose birth we all re-re-rejoice." She pulled a tiny wand from the folds of her gown, and from the wand came great flashes of silver as she waved it over the sleeping child. "I bear the g-gift of love, which she will give and r-r-receive generously."

A second fairy stepped forward. "Beauty of face and form are the gifts I bring. With every year that passes her loveliness will increase."

"She will be graceful as a gazelle, dancing through life on fairy feet," said the third woman.

"Better than beauty or grace, she will have a heart easily stirred to pity for things weak

9

and suffering, and the desire to improve, by her every deed, the world around her," was the promise of the fourth woman.

Then said the fifth: "The gift of true sight and hearing shall be hers, so that she may see beauty in all things and enjoy the eternal music of the wind and the waves."

"I bring her the gift of laughter which, like the sun's rays, lightens the darkest day." The bearer of this gift smiled down on the sleeping princess.

"Mine is the gift of wisdom, so that she may know the true value of the people and things around her," said a little woman, bent and aged.

The next fairy had a voice that was strong and sweet. "From water, sea and air I give her protection. Neither the fury of the storm nor the consuming heat of the sun will overcome her."

"Riches and wealth will she have, but she will use them wisely for her own happiness and for the good of others," said the ninth woman.

"Joy will be her companion every day that she lives," promised the next fairy.

The eleventh wise woman, the tallest and oldest of them all, began to walk up the steps towards the silk-draped cradle.

But before she could declare her gift a great flash of lightning lit up the windows of the hall, and a storm, more violent than any could remember, raged outside. As though they were indeed expecting another guest, the eyes of everyone present turned towards the heavy oak door. They saw that it had been blown open by a mighty gust of wind, and in the doorway stood the fairy whom nobody had remembered to invite.

She was a tall and stately figure, but her face with distorted and ugly with jealousy and hate.

"So this child is to be blessed above all others, to have beauty and wisdom, wealth and kindness. And joy, too, every day that she lives." The wise woman laughed loudly, and the faces of everyone present grew pale at the sound of that laughter.

"Yes, joy she shall have," continued the woman, "but her days will be few. This is *my* gift to this precious child. In her fifteenth year the king's daughter shall wound herself on a spindle and fall down dead."

In the dreadful silence that followed, the twelfth fairy, who had her gift still to give, bent over the baby's cradle.

"No words of mine can remove this terrible curse," she said sadly. "But with my power of magic I decree that this death which overcomes the king's daughter shall not be a real death, but only a hundred years' deep sleep. This is *my* gift."

The parents of the princess were overcome by dread and sorrow. Thinking to save his dear child from harm, the king sent out an order that every spindle in the kingdom should be burned. That very same evening a mighty holocaust rose up to the heavens as the people gladly complied with the wishes of their king. But the wicked fairy woman only laughed at the sight.

In the years that followed the gifts of the wise women were all fulfilled: for the girl was so beautiful, good, kind, and sensible that nobody who knew her could help loving her. Soon even her parents began to disbelieve that evil could ever befall so favoured a girl. Only her name reminded them of the fairy woman's curse. For she had been called Briar-Rose, and everyone knows that even the most beautiful rose bears a thorn.

12

The fifteenth birthday of the princess came and went without mishap. Now everyone was convinced that the woman's evil power had been thwarted.

So it was that, a few weeks after her birthday, the princess was left quite alone in the castle while her parents and the servants attended a great function in a nearby kingdom.

The girl was not lonely. She wandered happily through the rooms and chambers, many of which she had never before seen. At last she came to some narrow winding stairs that led up to an old tower. At the top of the steps was a little door, with a rusty key in the lock. When the princess turned the key the door sprang open and there, in a little dusty room, sat an old woman, busily spinning her flax on a spindle.

Briar-Rose had never seen a spindle before and, being a clever girl, she was fascinated by anything new.

"What sort of a thing is it that jumps about so gaily?" she asked the woman.

"Try it for yourself, my dear."

The princess sat down on the little stool. But she had hardly touched the spindle before the spell was fulfilled and she pricked her finger with it.

At the instant she felt the prick she fell down on the floor and lay in a deep sleep.

But the fairy who had changed the spell
of death into one of sleep, and who knew
that this accident must happen to the girl,
came now with her friends to the little room
in the tower. They carried Briar-Rose back
to her own bedroom in the castle and laid
her gently on the bed.

"Sleep softly, little princess, and dream
sweet dreams," said the good and wise
woman. "And so that you may not wake to
mourn your parents and friends in a strange
world, I will give you company in your long
sleep."

Even as she spoke, sleep spread over all
the castle.

The king and queen, who had just come home and entered the hall, began to go to sleep, and all the courtiers with them. The horses went to sleep in the stables, the dogs in the yard, the doves on the roof, the flies on the wall. Yes, even the fire that was flickering in the hearth grew still and went to sleep. The roast meat stopped spluttering; the maid stopped stirring the soup, sleeping as she stood; and the cook, who was going to give the boy a smart slap because he had forgotten to watch the sauce, let him go and slept. In the castle courtyard the wind was still, and no leaf stirred in the trees that grew there.

Then all around the castle rose a thick hedge of briars. It got higher every year until it surrounded the whole castle and grew up over it, so that nothing more could be seen of the castle on the hill, not even the flag on its roof.

16

In the farms and villages of the kingdom those who had known and loved the princess grew old and died. Others were born then and they too died, until at last there was nobody alive who could really prove that the castle had ever existed.

But the story was still told of the beautiful sleeping Briar-Rose, and from time to time kings' sons came and tried to get through the hedge and into the castle. But the briars, as though they had hands, clung fast together. The young men were imprisoned in the cruel tangles, and sometimes they could not get out again and they died a wretched death.

At last, after long, long years, a king's son, handsome and brave, came into that country. He listened to the story of the lovely Briar-Rose who lay sleeping in the hidden castle, surrounded by her parents and courtiers, who slept too.

"I will go and see the beautiful princess," declared the prince.

The old men warned him of the peril of the briar hedge and of the many who, in attempting to conquer it, had died sad deaths.

"I am not afraid," said the prince. "No hedge or barrier will keep me from Briar-Rose."

But now the hundred years were over, and the day had come when Briar-Rose was to wake again. So, when the King's son went up to the briars they became, suddenly, just great beautiful flowers that parted, of their own accord, before him and allowed him to pass through unhurt. Behind him they closed together into a green hedge again, neat and low.

In the castle courtyard the prince saw the horses and the mottled hounds as they sprawled, fast asleep; on the roof perched the doves, their heads stuck under their wings. When he entered the castle the flies were sleeping on the wall; in the kitchen the cook still held up his hand as though to hit the boy; and the maid stood sleeping, her hand still poised to stir the big cauldron of soup.

He walked, amazed, through the rooms of sleeping people. In the great hall he found all the courtiers lying at the tables and on the floor, asleep, and on their thrones slept the king and queen.

His footsteps echoed through the silent castle as he climbed the stairs. The bedrooms were all empty . . . until he came to the one where Briar-Rose lay.

The prince held his breath in wonder at her beauty. He could not take his eyes off the girl, who smiled so gently in her sleep. He bent down to kiss her and, just as he touched her with his lips, Briar-Rose awoke.

As Briar-Rose and the prince went downstairs together, the king awoke. The queen and all the courtiers woke up too, rubbing their eyes.

The horses in the courtyard got up and shook themselves; the hounds sprang up and wagged their tails; the doves on the roof pulled out their heads from under their wings and flew away; the flies on the wall began to crawl again; the fire in the kitchen started up with a great blaze to cook the dinner; the maid resumed her stirring of the soup, and the cook gave the boy a great box on the ear, a punishment that he had earned a hundred years before.

Amid scenes of great happiness and splendour, Briar-Rose married the king's son, And they lived happily till their lives' end.

NURSERY RHYMES

JACK AND JILL

Jack and Jill went up the hill
To fetch a pail of water;
But they were whisked up in the sky,
To live on the moon ever after.

A BUNCH OF BLUE RIBBONS

Oh dear, what can the matter be?
Oh dear, what can the matter be?
Oh dear, what can the matter be?
Johnny's so long at the fair.

He promised he'd buy me a
    bunch of blue ribbons,
He promised he'd buy me a
    bunch of blue ribbons,
He promised he'd buy me a
    bunch of blue ribbons,
To tie up my bonny brown hair.

THE UGLY DUCKLING

It was summer time on the farm, a lazy summer day when the yellow wheat swayed very gently and the cows in the meadow flicked their tails half-heartedly at the pestering flies. Down by the stream the drone of the bees provided a sleepy lullaby for the big farm dog who stretched out under the comparative cool of the shady beech tree.

Everyone on the farm, in fact, was at peace or asleep . . . except the mother duck. She was working very hard indeed, for it was time for her to hatch out her ducklings.

The afternoon was so hot, and hatching out was such a long job that she was beginning to lose patience. She longed to be swimming about in the cool stream with the other ducks.

Selfish things that they were, these friends of hers! They hardly ever thought of visiting her, though it would have passed the weary time happily for her if they would only have sat by her side for a while, having a quack with her. Selfish things, indeed!

The mother duck settled herself more comfortably on her eggs.

At last her patience was rewarded and the eggs cracked open, one after the other. Peep! Peep! Peep!

"*Quack, Quack!*" said the mother duck, pleased now with herself and the world.

It was worth all her long wait, she decided, as she surveyed the little balls of fluffy yellow fur

who were cautiously emerging from their shells.

But then she noticed something peculiar. One large egg, bigger than any of the others, was still sitting there, unbroken.

" However can that be?" wondered the mother duck. " Well, I haven't any patience to sit here any longer, anyway."

For her lively ducklings were already demanding to see the large world that lay on the other side of the meadow.

The mother duck wandered away a few steps; then she looked back. It was such a fine large egg, it really seemed a shame to leave it.

As she sat down again on the egg, her friends passed by from their swim. She explained the situation to them.

" I bet it's a turkey's egg," said an older duck. " I once had that trick played on me. *Quack! Quack!* The trouble I had with that young one. It just wouldn't swim. Afraid of the water, fancy that !"

They wandered off, leaving the mother duck all alone again with her impatient ducklings and the one unbroken egg.

At last the big egg cracked. " *Peep! Peep!*" went the young one as it tumbled out.

The baby was large and ugly, and grey in colour, quite unlike any of her other little golden duck-lings. The mother duck couldn't help feeling disappointed after all her trouble.

" Perhaps it *is* a turkey chick after all," said the mother duck. " Well, we shall soon see tomorrow."

The next day was fine and sunny and the mother
duck took her whole family down to the stream.
Splash! into the water she jumped.

"*Quack! Quack!*" she ordered them. And,
one by one, the ducklings plopped in after her.

As they hit the water all their little heads went
under it, but immediately they were up again and
floating along beautifully. Even the ugly grey
duckling gave a magnificent performance.

"Well, it's no turkey chick, that's certain,"
said the mother duck. "Indeed he swims very
gracefully. And, when you really come to look
at him, I think he becomes quite handsome."

Their swim over, the mother duck led her little
brood proudly into the farmyard to meet the
other animals.

"Keep close beside me," she warned them,
"for you're so tiny that some of the bigger animals
could easily tramp on you. And *do* beware of
Tom, the big black cat, for he's very greedy and
might just fancy a duckling for his tea."

The farm animals crowded round to greet the

new arrivals. There were ducks and hens, a rooster and some turkeys, proud animals who were born with spurs and who puffed up their feathers like a ship under full sail.

"Your ducklings are charming, my dear," said one of the turkeys condescendingly. "Except for this one. He's so gawky and peculiar that he'll have to be taught not to come near his betters."

"Leave him alone," said the mother duck. "He's a good-tempered duckling and he can swim even better than the others. I expect his looks will improve as he grows older."

But the poor duckling who was last out of the egg was so despised that he got pecked and pushed and scorned by all the animals on the farm.

Every day his life there became harder to bear, and even his own brothers and sisters treated him badly, laughing at him and leaving him out of their games.

The ducks nipped him, the hens pecked him and sometimes the girl who fed the poultry let fly at him with her foot.

Eventually the ugly duckling could bear it no longer. He ran away from the farm, flying off to the great marsh where the wild ducks lived.

The next morning he was wakened by the sound of shotguns. A big shoot was on and parties of men were spread all around the marsh, their gun dogs beside them.

The poor duckling just lay there shivering as shot after shot passed over his head. Then he looked up to see a great ravenous dog, with lolling tongue and greedy eyes, hovering above him.

But the dog passed on without touching him.

" It must be because I'm so ugly," sighed the duckling. " Even the dog doesn't fancy me."

He lay there all day quite still, while ducks were shot down all around him.

It was late in the day before everything was quiet again. And it was some hours after that, and quite dark, before the duckling dared to get up and look round him. Seeing no men with guns, he left the marsh as fast as he could.

Over field and meadow he scuttled all through that night and the following day.

It was evening again when he came to a broken-down farm cottage. The wind was howling and blowing so fiercely now that the little duckling was nearly blown to pieces.

As he cowered for shelter near the house, the door of the cottage was blown open by a great gust of wind. The duckling went gladly through it.

In the cottage an old woman lived with her cat and her hen. They were very superior animals and, although they knew nothing of the world beyond the broken-down cottage, they thought they knew everything about everything.

" Can you lay eggs?" the hen asked the duckling.

" No," admitted the duckling.

" Then hold your tongue, ugly thing," said the hen.

"Can you arch your back or purr?" asked the cat.

"No," admitted the duckling. "But I love to swim in the clear water, and to duck my head underneath it and swim to the bottom."

"Well, I never heard anything so ridiculous," clucked the hen. "Now the cat is the cleverest person I've ever met. Ask *her* if she's fond of swimming or diving. Ask the old woman, and she's the wisest woman in all the world."

"You don't understand," said the duckling, very upset.

"Now, put these foolish notions out of your head," said the hen, "and be glad of a nice warm home. And in return, learn to lay eggs and purr, so that you may repay our kindness."

The poor duckling didn't think he'd ever be clever enough to do either of these things. So he knew he'd have to go out into the world again.

And off he went !

He swam on streams and lakes, skimming over the surface with great grace and sometimes diving down to the bottom, just for fun.

He could have been happy. But no animal would have anything to do with him because of his ugliness, so he was very lonely.

He passed the summer months all by himself, a lone figure on the great lakes and marshes, always moving from one place to another in search of a friend.

But no friend could he find, for all despised and scorned his ugliness.

Autumn came. The skies became grey and frosty and the winds grew gusty, blowing all the yellowed leaves before them from the trees.

Even a raven, perched on a fence, began to feel the bite of the icy breath of late autumn.

"*Caw, Caw,*" he croaked, and he flew away, leaving nobody there but the poor duckling.

Then, one evening, the snow-filled sky was lit up by the great red ball of the receding sun.

As the duckling watched in awe this spectacle of nature, a great flock of large handsome birds appeared out of the bushes. They were swans. But the duckling had never seen such birds, with their magnificent sweeping wings, all glittering white, and their long powerful necks.

As he watched in wonder, they uttered a weird but beautiful cry and, spreading out their strong wings, they flew from this cold country to dwell on open lakes in warmer lands.

They soared higher and higher into the air as the little duckling continued to watch them. He could not take his gaze away from them. He turned round and round in the water like a wheel, craning his neck in their direction and uttering a cry so shrill and strange that it scared even himself.

He knew he could never forget these beautiful birds. He knew not what they were called, nor where they were flying, yet they were dearer to him than anything he had ever seen.

Still he didn't envy them, nor did he seek to join them. How could he, the ugliest of ugly ducklings, expect to be accepted by such lovely creatures? If only the ducks would be friends with him *he* would be satisfied.

It grew colder and colder each day as autumn changed into winter.

The duckling had to keep swimming about in a circle now to prevent the water from freezing up. But every night the pool he was swimming in grew smaller and smaller and the ice froze so hard that you could hear it creaking.

One day he swam about so fiercely—trying to prevent the pool from closing up altogether—that, at last, faint from exhaustion and cold, he lay quite still and froze fast in the ice.

A farmer, passing the pond next morning, found him. He carried the poor duckling home to his wife.

In the comforting heat the duckling revived and the man's children were thrilled with their new pet.

They wanted to play with him, but the duckling, thinking they intended to hurt him—as he had seen those men with their guns hurt his kind—fluttered wildly about the room.

He spilled the big jug of milk, flew into the butter tub and then fell into the flour bin.

What a sight he looked!

The children shouted with laughter. The farmer's wife chased round after him angrily, and the poor duckling circled round and round until at last he found the open window.

Out he flew and into the bushes to sink down, dazed, in the cold white snow.

It was a cold and lonely winter for the poor duckling sheltering, all alone, among the reeds of the marsh.

But one morning he awoke to find the sky clear again. There was something different about today, even the half-starved duckling could sense it: an air of new life and expectancy, of hope and promise.

Now the larks were singing and one or two birds had already begun to make their nests.

The duckling began to feel that life was a joyful thing.

Stretching himself, he tried his wings. The *whirr* of them was louder than before; they were stronger, too, and now they carried him swiftly away.

Up and up he flew, across the waters of the lake, now quiet, but which he well remembered in all its winter fury.

Across fields still bleak and brown he flew, until eventually he came to a garden where apple and cherry trees were in blossom and fragrant lilac blooms dipped, from their long green boughs, into a winding stream.

It was quiet and peaceful here, filled with all the fresh and sweet-smelling beauty of spring.

Then, straight ahead, out of the thicket, sailed three beautiful white swans, ruffling their feathers as they floated so lightly on the water. The duckling recognised these splendid creatures and they made him feel strangely sad.

Then, all at once, he knew his destiny.

"I will fly across to these wonderful birds," he thought. "No doubt they will pick me to death for daring to approach them, ugly as I am."

"But I am prepared for that," the duckling thought. "I would prefer to be killed by them than be nipped by the ducks, pecked by the hens, kicked by the girl who feeds the poultry, and endure another winter, cold and alone, by the lakeside."

So the ugly duckling flew out on to the water. Swiftly and surely he swam towards the graceful swans.

Catching sight of him they darted, ruffling their feathers, to meet him.

But the duckling felt neither fear nor despair, only a calm acceptance.

"Yes, kill me, kill me!" he cried, and he bowed his head to the water, awaiting death.

But what did he see there in the clear stream? It was a reflection of himself, but so different from the clumsy grey bird, ugly and unattractive, that he remembered. Now he was himself a swan! And the three great swans, instead of scorning and killing him, swam round and round and stroked him with their beaks.

Soon some children came into the garden and threw bread and grain into the water for the birds to eat.

"There's a new swan," one of them called out.

The children crowded round to see him, throwing bread and cakes into the water and clapping their hands in delight.

They fetched their mother and father to admire the new swan and everyone said: " The new one is the prettiest. He's so young and handsome."

The lilac trees lowered their branches into the water before him as he swam, and the sun shone down warmly on his graceful white back. And the old swans bowed before him.

He felt quite shy at all this attention and he tucked his head under his wings.

Then he thought of how he had been despised and persecuted and now—although he felt no different—he was said by everyone to be the loveliest of birds.

He was happy but not a bit proud, for he, who had once been the ugly duckling, knew so well that pride was a foolish thing.

He was glad too that he had suffered such hardship and want. For it had taught him wisdom and tolerance and made him appreciate all the more the happiness and beauty that life now offered him.

LITTLE JACK HORNER

Little Jack Horner
Sat in a corner,
Eating his Christmas pie;
He put in his thumb,
And pulled out a plum,
And said,
" What a good boy am I!"

LITTLE POLLY FLINDERS

Little Polly Flinders
Sat among the cinders,
Warming her pretty little toes!
Her mother came and caught her,
And whipped her little daughter
For spoiling her nice new clothes.

ROCK-A-BYE, BABY

Rock-a-bye, baby, on the tree top!
When the wind blows,
    the cradle will rock;
When the bough breaks,
    the cradle will fall;
Down will come baby, cradle and all.

LITTLE BOY BLUE

Little Boy Blue, come blow your horn!
The sheep's in the meadow, the cow's in the corn.
Where is the little boy who looks after the sheep?
He's under the haystack, fast asleep.
Will you wake him? No, not I!
For if I do, he's sure to cry.

Snow White
AND THE SEVEN DWARFS

ONCE upon a time a baby was born to the King and Queen of a faraway land. She was named Snow White and all the fairies of the land attended her christening. They brought the child great gifts of beauty, and even more precious gifts of a kind heart and a loving nature.

So the child grew into a beautiful girl. And she was loved by all who knew her.

Her mother and father having died, Snow White now lived with her stepmother, Marian, a woman of great beauty but cruel and cold of heart. Evil and jealous, she knew some of the black craft of witches. Her dearest possession was a magic mirror which constantly assured her of her beauty.

Until one day . . .

"Mirror, mirror, on the wall,
Who is the fairest one of all?"

She waited, smiling, for the expected answer.

But this time the mirror replied

"Through all the land
    for many years
Your beauty won you fame;
But now a lovelier maid there is
And Snow White is her name."

Marian's face grew ugly with hatred and anger. The girl must die.

Calling a huntsman, she bribed him with gold and silver, and ordered him to take Snow White into the deep woods and slay her.

"And bring me her heart that I may know the deed has been done as I commanded it," said the cunning Marian, for she feared the man might take pity on the girl and let her live.

And so it happened. For, try as he would, the huntsman could not find it in his heart to kill this girl whose only fault lay in her loveliness, which had aroused the hatred of a wicked woman.

"Run away, far away" he told her, as he confessed to the dreadful deed which he had been ordered to do. "And always take care that no word ever reaches your stepmother that you still live, for she would surely put an end to both of us with her own hands."

Leaving her in the forest he returned to the castle. On his way he killed a young boar so that he might present its heart to Marian as proof of Snow White's death.

Alone among the tall trees, Snow White was frightened of the dark shadows and of the unseen creatures that lurked in them. But no animals attacked her. The timid rabbits and squirrels and the gentle deer were, at first, more frightened of her than she was of them. The little birds, seeing her fear, sang sweet songs to cheer her and they led her at last to a clearing in the middle of the big forest.

It was just before nightfall and, by the last rays of the sun, she could see at the far side of the clearing a pretty little house of red brick with a roof of gaily coloured tiles.

She walked up the little path leading to the front door.

"Rat-a-tat-tat." The sound of her knocking echoed through the quiet clearing.

She waited, but there was no reply. All was silent inside the little house.

So Snow White turned the handle and walked right in.

Just inside the door was a little round table, so low that at first Snow White thought it must be a little girl's toy. But then she noticed that it was set with seven places, and around it were seven tiny chairs. The owners of the chairs had eaten a meal there lately, with bread and butter and golden honey. And they had not waited to wash the dishes either.

Snow White noticed too that although there was à bowl of flowers on the table, the tablecloth was frayed and a little torn and cobwebs hung in all the corners of the room. So she guessed that no woman lived in the little house.

Quickly Snow White got to work and soon the dirty dishes were shining and the little room was spotless, its furniture polished and its corners swept.

Then Snow White saw some wooden steps at one corner of the room. Climbing up she found they led to a funny little attic bedroom in which seven beds stood side by side along the wall.

As she was very tired Snow White lay across the tiny beds and fell fast asleep.

It was quite dark and Snow White was still asleep when the seven little men returned from their work in the gold mine under the big hill.

They were astonished to find the fire lit, the kettle boiling and the table set with clean dishes. They searched the house until they found Snow White.

The seven little men tiptoed up to the girl and looked and looked. They had never imagined anybody could be so lovely.

At last Snow White woke up.

She looked in surprise at the little men, but she wasn't at all afraid of them for they looked so kind.

"I'm Snow White" she told them. "I do hope you don't mind me sleeping on your beds. I felt so tired!"

"A pleasure, Princess!" said the little man with bright red hair. He spoke slowly and solemnly in a deep voice that sounded odd coming from such a tiny person. "My name is Sunday and these are my brothers: Monday, Tuesday, Wednesday, Thursday, Friday and Saturday."

Snow White laughed. "But those are the days of the week."

"Well you see, Princess, we were named after the days on which we were born. This was so that our parents could remember which of us was the oldest. Monday came first. You can always recognise him because he looks as miserable as a washday."

Snow White laughed as a little man with a long white beard blushed and hid behind his brother.

One by one the little men were introduced to her. Tuesday, Wednesday and Thursday, who looked exactly alike; Friday, who didn't like fish, and Saturday, who always looked rosy-pink as though he'd just had a bath.

"And of course anyone would know you were Sunday" Snow White remarked to the little man with red hair. "Your voice is just like that of a preacher in church."

When Snow White told them her story they begged her to stay in their house for as long as she liked.

So Snow White lived happily in the house of the seven dwarfs. She cleaned and cooked for them and washed their clothes. And every morning she waved goodbye as they marched off to the gold mine.

48

Back at the castle Marian's bitter disappointment and anger that her beauty could be challenged had kept her away from the mirror for many weeks.

But one morning, secure in the knowledge of Snow White's death, she again approached the mirror.

"Mirror, mirror, on the wall,
Who is the fairest one of all?"

The mirror answered

"Oh Queen, your beauty is full bright,
But fairer far is still Snow White
Who deep in the dark woods doth dwell,
With seven dwarfs who love her well."

Filled with fury that she had been so easily cheated, Marian determined that this time she would kill the girl herself. Disguising herself as an old beggar woman she set out for the house of the seven dwarfs, carrying on her arm a basket of apples. The shining red fruit looked delicious, but in one of the apples was a deadly poison.

When Snow White opened the door the old woman held out to her the nicest apple in the basket.

"Only the best is fitting for one so beautiful," she said.

Snow White hesitated, remembering the dwarfs' warnings.

But the old woman pleaded "I have walked over hills and dusty roads to bring you this fruit."

Not wishing to seem ungrateful Snow White took the apple. But at the very first bite she gasped and fell to the floor.

Hours later the dwarfs, returning from their work, found her still lying there. Her skin was warm and her breath came gently, as though she slept. But all their efforts failed to awaken her.

All was sadness in the little house for many days. Finally the little men lost hope of her recovery, so they made a coffin of glass with a golden frame. Laying Snow White in it they placed it in a shady spot beneath a blossoming tree.

Through the long summer days Snow White lay in her glass coffin.

Never was she alone. During the warm evenings the little men kept a constant vigil beside her. When they went to their work under the mountain the animals took their places: the deer, the rabbits and even an antlered buck; while birds sung above her all through the day. And Snow White remained beautiful as ever, peaceful in her deep sleep.

Summer passed and the leaves of autumn fell about the coffin. Later the winter snows heaped about it and frost made strange patterns on the glass.

In spring the birds returned from the warm southern lands where they had wintered. From these far-off countries they brought new seeds so that soon wonderful flowers, such as never before grew in these quiet woods, peeped up round about the coffin.

Then one day a Prince came riding by. Again and again he returned to keep his vigil of love with the seven dwarfs and the animals of the forest. He begged the little men to allow him to take the coffin back to his palace.

"Oh! we could not possibly allow that," boomed Sunday. "Why we would all miss her so much and we do look after her very well, you know."

But as the Prince grew sadder and paler week by week the kindhearted little men at last consented.

As the glass coffin was carried away the jolt loosened the piece of apple which had lodged in Snow White's throat and, the poison gone, she woke from her long sleep.

The awakening of Snow White brought great joy to the forest. The seven dwarfs rejoiced, as did all the animals who had loved and watched over her so tenderly.

The Prince, who had fallen in love with the sleeping girl, asked her to be his wife.

Snow White was married with great celebrations and the wicked stepmother was banished forever from the kingdom. With her Prince, Snow White lived happily for many years and they often visited the seven little men and their animal and bird friends of the forest.

HEIDI

THE morning was clear and bright, as a young woman and a girl, walking hand in hand, climbed up the steep path among the Swiss mountains. The child was wearing two dresses and a thick red shawl, on her feet were sturdy walking shoes.

After about an hour's climbing they reached a tiny village which lay between the valley and the Alm. The young woman had been born in this village and she was greeted by many friends as they passed through the narrow street.

" Where are you taking the girl, Dete? " asked one woman. " She's your dead sister's child, isn't she? "

" She is," replied Dete. " And I'm taking her up to the Alm Uncle. I've looked after Heidi ever since her parents died. Now I am going away to a good job, so the Alm Uncle must look after his son's child."

"I'll come along with you to Peter the goatherd's cottage," called Barbel. "His mother does some sewing for me."

As they walked along, the two women talked about Heidi's grandfather, whom everybody called the Alm Uncle because he lived all alone on top of the Alm. He was a very old man, over seventy years, and he lived like a hermit, speaking to nobody for months on end. As a young man, the Alm Uncle had been wealthy, having a fine farm in the valley below. But he had been foolish and frittered away all his money. Then his only son, Heidi's father, had been killed in an accident. After that the old man had gone to live up the Alm, getting more surly and bad-tempered as the years passed, or so it was said.

"I wouldn't be in Heidi's shoes for anything," said Barbel, before they parted. "The child will be terrified of that old horror with his bushy eyebrows and tangled beard."

But Heidi was not troubled by any such fears. As the two young women had been walking along slowly, chatting as they went, Peter the goatherd had caught up with them. Heidi had run on ahead with the eleven-year-old boy whom she had met on previous visits to the village with her aunt.

Peter was driving his goats far up the mountain, where there was fresh grass and herbs in plenty for them to eat. At dusk he would collect his little herd and return back down to the village with them.

Heidi looked wistfully at the boy's bare feet and scanty clothes. He skipped nimbly along, while she was hampered by her heavy, clumsy clothes.

Suddenly she sat down on the ground and pulled off her shoes, stockings and the thick shawl. Next she slipped off the Sunday dress which her aunt had put on over the light everyday dress which Heidi usually wore.

Now she was free. Laughing with joy, she did a little dance in her bare feet.

Peter watched the little girl in amusement. Then bundling her discarded clothing into the shawl, he slung it on a stick which he carried across his shoulder.

"Whatever made you take off your clothes and shoes?" scolded Dete when her friend had gone.

"I didn't need them," said Heidi simply.

About an hour later they came within sight of the Alm. The hut of the Alm Uncle stood on an overhanging ledge of the mountain with three great pine trees behind it; and beyond them rose the mountains, sheer and cold. Exposed to all the fury of the winter winds, the hut got its share of summer sunshine, too.

It was like living in an eyrie on top of the world; below was the valley full of laughing, busy people, and here, on a bench outside his lonely hut, sat an old man, quietly smoking his pipe as he watched his visitors approaching.

Reaching the top first, Heidi ran to the old man, laid her little hand in his, and said, " Good day, Grandfather."

Taken aback, the old man hesitated. But then he shook hands gravely with the child.

" Good day, Uncle," Dete greeted him briskly. " I don't suppose you recognise Heidi — you haven't seen her since she was a year old. Since then I've done my duty by her. Now you can do yours. The child must stay with *you* now."

" A child—here—" growled the Alm Uncle. " If she cries and frets for you, what shall I do with her?"

" Heidi is a good child," replied Dete. " She will be no trouble to you. And you will answer for it if harm comes to her."

Taking leave of the child quickly, Dete fled down the mountain before the old man could raise further objections.

60

" I'd like to see the inside of the hut, Grand-father," said Heidi, as the old man continued to smoke in silence.

" Come along then and take your bundle," he said, pointing to the clothes which Peter had left beside Heidi.

" I won't need them anymore," announced Heidi.

" Why not? " asked the old man.

" Goats don't have a lot of clothes to bother them," replied Heidi. " I'd rather be like the goats."

The old man didn't argue but led her into the one large room of the hut. There was a table and chair in the middle of the floor, a large kettle hung over the hearth and against one wall was the bunk on which the old man slept.

" Where shall I sleep, Grandfather? " asked Heidi.

" Where you please," he replied.

Heidi saw a small ladder. Climbing up it she entered the hayloft. The floor was strewn with sweet-smelling hay and from the little round window Heidi could look down upon the whole valley.

" Oh, this is lovely, Grandfather," she cried in delight. " I shall sleep here."

Together Heidi and the Alm Uncle made up a bed of the soft hay on which the old man spread an old but clean sack. Then he found a long piece of cloth for a sheet to cover the girl.

" It's a lovely bed," cried Heidi when they had finished.

" We must eat now," said the Alm Uncle.

As the old man toasted cheese over the fire Heidi found knives and plates in a large cupboard, also a loaf of bread, which she put on the table.

" You are a sensible child," nodded the Alm Uncle approvingly. " You do things for yourself without having to be told."

He brought over a three-legged stool that stood by the hearth and lifted the little girl up on it. Together they ate their meal of bread and cheese with the sweet goat's milk.

That evening Peter came again to bring the goats down from the mountain. Two of the goats belonged to the Alm Uncle.

" The white one is Little Swan and the brown one is Little Bear," the Alm Uncle told Heidi.

The Alm Uncle milked the white goat and filled a bowl with the milk.

" Here is your supper, child," he said. " I must put the goats into the stall, so go to bed and sleep well."

" Goodnight, Grandfather. Goodnight, Little Swan. Goodnight, Little Bear," cried Heidi.

Soon she curled up in the warm hay and slept as sweetly as any princess among silken sheets.

Heidi awakened to find the sun streaming through the little window above her bed. Happiness flooded over her when she remembered where she was and she jumped up, eager for the new day to begin.

Peter was standing outside the hut with his flock.

" Would you like to go up to the pasture with the Goat-General? " her grandfather asked her.

" Oh, yes, please," cried Heidi, and she ran to wash herself in the big tub of rainwater that stood at the door of the hut.

The Alm Uncle gave Peter a big slice of cheese, some bread and milk.

" You must take care of Heidi," he warned the boy.

The mountain slopes were bathed in golden sunshine that day and everywhere bright flowers grew in such profusion as Heidi had never imagined.

In the middle of the morning they sat down to rest in the pasture and they ate their meal with hearty appetites, while Peter told Heidi the names of all his goats.

" The prettiest of all are Little Swan and Little Bear," said Heidi.

That night, alone in the hut with her Grandfather, Heidi talked about her lovely day.

" There was a big eagle, Grandfather," she said, " and as he rose in the air he screamed so loudly. Why does he scream so? "

The old man's face changed. " He is jeering at the people who pass their miserable lives in the crowded towns and villages below, huddled together like sheep and making one another wretched," he said, and his voice was harsh and bitter.

Heidi was frightened by his tone. But presently she asked him, " Grandfather, when the day is ending the sun turns red and everything seems to be on fire. Where does all the fire come from? "

Her grandfather's voice was soft and gentle now. " It's like this, child," he said. " When the sun says goodnight to the mountains he spills over them his loveliest colours so that they will not forget him until he returns in the morning."

This beautiful picture pleased the little girl and she went to sleep that night thinking about the great red ball of sun.

As the summer passed Heidi grew as brown as a berry. Then came autumn and one morning Heidi looked out of her little window and saw that a dazzling white cloak of snow covered the Alm.

Peter did not come up the mountain very often now, for during the winter he attended school every day.

But one day he came to Heidi with an invitation. " Granny would like you to come and see her, Heidi," he said.

So the next day the Alm Uncle tucked Heidi up warmly in his sled and they slid down the mountainside to the goatherd's cottage.

Heidi went into the cottage alone while her grandfather returned home.

In the tiny cottage a woman was sewing and, in the corner, a little old lady was spinning flax.

Heidi walked over to the spinning wheel. "Good day, Granny," she said. "It is Heidi—here I am."

"The child that lives with the Alm Uncle," said the old lady in a quavering voice. "Tell me, Brigida, what does she look like?"

"But I am here, Granny," said Heidi. "Look at me."

"I cannot see you, child," answered the old lady. "I am blind."

Heidi covered her face with her hands and cried. "Oh, Granny, Granny, can't anyone make you see again?"

"Do not upset yourself, child," said the old lady. "When one cannot see a loving face, it brings even more pleasure to hear a kindly word. You have made me very happy."

Heidi dried her eyes. But she made up her mind that she would tell her grandfather everything. He would make Granny see again and he would mend the windows to stop them rattling so loudly, and paint the cottage so that it would be bright and fresh.

That night at supper Heidi tackled the Alm Uncle.

"Grandfather, tomorrow we must take the nails and hammer and fix Granny's cottage so that it doesn't rattle anymore. No one can help her but you."

The Alm Uncle said nothing for a few moments, looking into the eyes of the child who trusted him so unquestioningly.

"Yes, we will go tomorrow, Heidi," he said.

And he kept his promise, doing his work so well that even when the fiercest winds blew, the walls and shutters no longer groaned and creaked.

During the winter Heidi visited the old, blind grandmother many times, bringing new joy and laughter into her life.

The years passed happily for Heidi and her grandfather until one summer day, when Heidi was nearly eight years old, a visitor arrived at the hut. It was Dete, smartly dressed and with a jaunty feather in her hat.

She had come for Heidi, she explained. The rich family for whom she worked had an invalid daughter of about Heidi's age for whom they wanted a companion. It would be a great opportunity for the child; she would be treated as their own daughter and would receive a good education, too.

"Why, there isn't a soul in the world who wouldn't thank Heaven for such a splendid piece of luck," finished Dete.

"Then they can have it," said the Alm Uncle angrily, "for the child and I want none of it."

"Heidi is nearly eight years old, yet she can neither read nor write," burst out Dete furiously. "Pack your clothes, Heidi, and come along with me."

At first Heidi refused to go but, when the Alm Uncle left the hut, Dete persuaded the little girl, telling her that she could soon return to her grandfather and bring back fine presents both for him and for the blind Granny.

Life at the large house where Dete worked was very different from what Heidi had become used to in the Alm Uncle's hut. Here there were servants to wait on you at table, with fancy food to eat and a high bed to sleep on with fine linen sheets.

But there was no little window through which Heidi could look out and see the whole valley spread out below her, green and sun-dappled in the summer months and like a scene from a Christmas card in winter, when the lights from the village shone up from the snow-covered slopes below.

Here Heidi looked out of her bedroom window on to an endless procession of roofs and chimneys, grey and sad-looking, belching smoke into the grey skies above.

The running of the house itself was left mostly to a stern housekeeper and Heidi found that there were rules for everything—for going to bed and getting up, for eating and walking, for speaking and keeping silent.

The two girls got on well together. Clara, who was twelve, had been in a wheelchair all her life and the lively little girl brought fun and laughter into her rather dull life.

But Heidi was not happy in the big city. Wherever she looked she saw only walls and windows, grey pavements instead of green grass, withering window boxes instead of the gay flowers that grew in profusion on her beloved mountains.

There were happy moments, of course, for life is never wholly dark. Heidi learned to read, and a little book containing pictures and stories about animals became her most cherished possession.

But, although the little girl enjoyed her new interests, her dark eyes were often sad. Finally she could not force herself to eat the dainty foods set before her by the kind servants to tempt her appetite. Each day she grew paler and thinner and at night she would cry herself to sleep, muffling her sobs in the pillow.

At last the family doctor was called in. He examined Heidi and then questioned the child gently.

" Do you like living here, Heidi? " he asked.

" Everyone is very kind to me and I love Clara," replied Heidi.

" But are you happy, child? "

Heidi could not answer.

" Did you not find it lonely in the Alm with only an old man for company? " asked the doctor.

" Oh, no, it was beautiful there." Heidi sobbed heartbrokenly at the thought of all her friends there, and the goats, and her dear little bed of straw under the wonderful window from which she could see the whole world.

There was only one way to cure Heidi, the doctor told the family. She must be sent home at once to the Alm Uncle, for the disease from which the little girl was wasting away was homesickness.

Clara was sad at the parting but her parents promised they would take her to visit Heidi the following summer.

All the pretty dresses and clothes that had been bought for Heidi were packed in a wicker basket; there were presents too: for the Alm Uncle and the old, blind Granny and, of course, one for Peter the goatherd.

At last the long journey was over. Flushed with happiness, her eyes bright again, Heidi ran up the mountain path.

Now she could see the hut and seated on the bench smoking his pipe—just as he had been when she had first seen him—was the lonely figure of the Alm Uncle.

" Grandfather ! Dear Grandfather ! " cried Heidi, and the old man lifted her onto his knee, his arms encircling her joyfully. He, who had not cried for years, wept openly now.

His Heidi had come home. They would start a new life together. During the summer months they would stay up in the mountains but in the cold winters they would live in the village and Heidi would go to school with the other children.

Hand in hand, the old man and the little girl went into the hut. And Heidi slept well that night, her sleep filled with happy dreams.

NURSERY RHYMES

TO BED ! TO BED !

" To bed ! To bed !"
Says Sleepy-head.
" Let's stay awhile," says Slow.
" Put on the pan,"
Says greedy Nan,
" Let's sup before we go."

POLLY, PUT THE KETTLE ON

Polly, put the kettle on,
Polly, put the kettle on,
Polly, put the kettle on,
And let's drink tea.

Sukey, take it off again,
Sukey, take it off again,
Sukey, take it off again,
They're all gone away.

73

CURLY-LOCKS

Curly-locks! Curly-locks!
    Wilt thou be mine?
Thou shalt not wash dishes,
    nor yet feed swine;
But sit on a cushion,
    and sew a fine seam
And feed upon strawberries,
    sugar, and cream!

I LOVE LITTLE PUSSY

I love little pussy, her coat is so warm,
And if I don't hurt her, she'll do me no harm;
I'll not pull her tail nor drive her away,
But pussy and I very gently will play.

SIMPLE SIMON

Simple Simon met a pieman
    Going to the fair;
Said Simple Simon to the pieman,
    " Let me taste your ware."

Said the pieman to Simple Simon,
    " Show me first your penny."
Said Simple Simon to the pieman,
    " Indeed, I haven't any."

Cinderella

LONG, long ago, in a faraway land of magic and fairies, lived Cinderella. As her parents were dead, Cinderella lived with stepsisters who, jealous of her loveliness, treated her as a servant.

But Cinderella smiled as she worked. Somewhere, she knew, the sun shone and birds sang, so banishing all sad thoughts she made a wish on each bright soapy bubble and made friends of all the lowly creatures who spent as much time as she did on the big stone floors.

The little mice peeped out of their holes to admire the beautiful girl whose gentleness left them unafraid, and even the lizards did not scurry into hiding at her approach.

Thus time passed, with dreams and wishes but little joy for Cinderella. Until the day of the Palace ball. . . .

The King was holding a grand ball to honour his only son and all the ladies of the kingdom were to be invited. It was said that the Prince intended to choose his bride at the ball, so the stepsisters waited eagerly for their invitations.

"Here's one for you too, Cinders," sneered Mirabelle. "What will you wear, dear, your tattered grey or your patchwork black?"

"How I wish I could go," sighed Cinderella.

"Back to work, girl," snapped Miranda, "and earn your keep. You will have plenty to do later."

Their selfish demands kept Cinderella running back and forth all day as Miranda and Mirabelle preened and flounced before their mirrors to decide what they would wear. As their excitement mounted so did their jealous bickering become more bitter.

"You are not to wear that purple velvet, Mirabelle. It makes my pink satin look insipid."

"Those rubies ill become you, Miranda dear. Your skin looks so blotchy against their fineness."

So it continued until, gowned in splendour, powdered and perfumed, they were ready to depart.

But even the beauty of sparkling jewels and the flattery of fabrics and furs could not hide the discontent and spite which made them old and ugly. And they looked with jealous envy at Cinderella in whom the beauty of goodness shone like a flawless star.

After they had gone Cinderella sat wearily before the fire, watching the glowing cinders darken and die. Only the scratching of a mouse in search of a new home disturbed the silence in the big kitchen.

"I wish, oh how I wish that I could go to the ball," sighed Cinderella aloud.

As she spoke the air was filled with sweet music and a fairy appeared in the doorway, wand in hand.

"I am Rowena, Fairy of Wishes. I come, at your bidding, from the Land of Dreams and I have power to grant all desires, big and small."

"How wonderful," breathed Cinderella. "But I have wished many times before and you have not come to me."

"The Land of Dreams lies far beyond the rainbow, in the Valley of the Burning Sun. It is only when people wish very hard that I can hear them."

The fairy set to work and soon Cinderella

was transformed into a dream of loveliness in a gown of pink silk, delicate as the petals of a rose and embroidered with crystals blue as a summer sky. Her headdress was of silver, spun by a fairy spider, and her veil, transparent as moonlight, was bordered with petals which bathed her in sweet perfume.

"Beautiful, my dear, really beautiful," murmured the fairy in satisfaction. "Now this green pumpkin, large and juicy, shall become your coach. Faced with silver and lined with satin, its beauty will match that of Cinderella, a fitting carriage to take her to the ball."

The fairy paused. "But what of a driver, and horses and coachmen? Bring me your friends, Cinderella, that they may serve you as friends should."

Cinderella sadly confessed to having not even one friend.

But, even as she spoke, a little voice piped up and six little mice and three lizards came to offer their help.

Flying stars and flashes of golden light filled the air as the fairy performed the magic that turned six mice into prancing grey horses, spotted white. A lizard, green and fat, became a stately coachman, in livery of royal purple with red plumed hat, while the other lizards became pages to ride at the back of the splendid coach.

"Now to the ball!" the fairy said. "But remember, all magic ends upon the witching hour of twelve. So leave, my dear, before the clock ceases its toll, for as the last note fades then will your riches turn to rags again and the fair Princess will once more become the servant girl."

Having said this, the fairy disappeared.

The coachman cracked his whip and the horses tip-tapped daintily along, their red plumes dancing merrily.

Clippety clop! Clippety clop! through the grey sleeping streets of the town sped the shining coach, past shuttered houses whose lights dimmed and flickered out as they sped past.

Then, against a sky that shone silvery in the moonlight, Cinderella glimpsed a fairytale castle of minarets and graceful spires. It stood high on a hill, its tall battlements seeming to reach into the skies above.

It was ablaze with light, ringing with music and laughter.

With a fanfare of trumpets Cinderella entered the ballroom.

She stood quite still for a moment, gazing around in happy amazement.

Inside, the scene was more wonderful than anything she had ever dreamed. The bright lights that hung from the ceiling were like dewdrops from a rainbow. The carpets were soft and springy, like walking on a bed of moss, and on the walls were mirrors so large that they reflected all the gay profusion of colour that filled the ballroom. Red, blue and green, purple, yellow and orange, mingled together in a vast sea of colour. With the flash of diamonds, rubies and emeralds, Cinderella was so dazzled that, for a moment, she closed her eyes.

When she opened her eyes again it was still the same bright scene. Then Cinderella knew that this was all really happening to her, no dream could ever be as beautiful as this night.

She thought gratefully of the Fairy Rowena, who had made all this come true. She must enjoy every moment of each precious hour.

As soft music played, Cinderella slowly descended the big staircase.

Catching sight of her the ladies below ceased their chattering to stare at her curiously from behind their fans.

"But who is she, my dear, do you know?"

"She must surely be a Princess. But somebody must know her. . . ."

"I have never seen her before for I would surely remember her."

After a moment of echoing silence they began to talk again, their rapid exciting twittering sounding like a crowd of magpies.

But nobody recognised Cinderella, not even her stepsisters. Although . . .

"There is something about that girl reminds me . . ." said Mirabelle.

"Yes," said Miranda slowly. "But how absurd of us . . . to compare a Princess with our Cinders!"

The Prince too gazed at the girl, whose beauty captured his heart.

The Prince and Cinderella danced together as the hours sped by and the girl was so happy that she almost forgot the warning of the Fairy Rowena.

"One, two, three." The loud chimes sounded over the music.

"How time has fled, my dear," murmured the Prince. "Already the clock strikes the midnight hour."

"Four, five, six, seven, eight."

Suddenly Cinderella remembered.

How could she have forgotten that for her each joyous moment was numbered?

Panic-stricken, she ran from the ballroom, not even waiting to bid the Prince goodbye.

On she raced, up the wide marble staircase. Past the staring dancers and through the palace door she ran, before the astonished footmen could offer to summon her carriage.

The Prince called out as he tried to catch up with the fleeing girl. But Cinderella was deaf now to everything but the warning sound of the church bells.

"Nine, ten, eleven."

They clanged like thunder in her ears as she ran on, heedless of the sharp stones that cut her bare foot.

At last she had reached the safety of the palace gate and, breathless now, she paused and listened for the last note. And as it sounded all the fairy's words came true.

So the footmen coming out, at the Prince's command, to search for a beautiful Princess saw only a poor servant girl. None of them noticed how the girl limped as she walked along. For on one foot she still wore a silken slipper. The second slipper she had lost as she ran so fearfully up the palace stairs.

Through all the land the Prince searched for his lost Princess. He proclaimed his love to all the nation and declared his wish to marry the girl if she could be found.

But though many came forward claiming to be the Princess, each claim was recognised as false by the unhappy Prince.

All day long street criers went through every town in the kingdom asking that the favoured girl come forward to grant the Prince's dearest wish.

"What on earth can the wretched girl be thinking about?" asked Miranda enviously. "Fancy ignoring an offer of marriage from the Prince!"

"There can be no such Princess," said Mirabelle. "I think she must have been a witch sent to torment him. The Prince would do well to forget her and choose his bride elsewhere."

"And I suppose you think he'd choose you," snapped Miranda jealously.

Cinderella listened unhappily, but she dared not come forward. For who would believe that the ragged servant girl had been, for one night, the dream-bride of a Prince?

In a silent palace the Prince sat, hour after weary hour, staring at a tiny slipper, his only remembrance of the girl he had hoped would share his throne.

One day, as he sat thus, a thought came to him. Quickly he called his servants and instructed them to go into every house in the land and find the one whom the slipper fitted.

"And bring her to me at once," the Prince said, "for she shall be my bride."

"Our poor Prince is mad with grief," the servants murmured, "for there will be hundreds whom the slipper fits."

But they soon found that the slipper was a magic one which stretched to great lengths on some and became so tight and constricting on others that they screamed with pain.

At last the page arrived at the home of Cinderella.

As Cinderella watched, the stepsisters shoved and struggled, puffed and panted in a vain effort to make the slipper fit. Two mice, who had been pages on that magic night, looked on in merry glee and Cinderella could not help but laugh too.

"Now it is your turn," the page told Cinderella.

"She is but a servant girl," protested Miranda.

"It is the Prince's command that every lady in the land shall fit the slipper," the page replied.

Cinderella slipped her foot easily into the magic slipper and from her pocket she took out the second slipper, which she had carried with her ever since the ball.

The stepsisters were speechless with astonishment as Cinderella left in the royal carriage. But the girl was too happy and too kind-hearted to bear a grudge, so she forgave them for all their unkindness to her.

And as she entered the palace a wonderful thing happened. Visible only to Cinderella, the Fairy Rowena appeared and, with a wave of her wand, Cinderella was dressed again in all her splendour of the ball.

The Prince was overjoyed to have found her at last and they planned to marry very soon.

The bells of the kingdom rang out merrily. But this time they held no fear for Cinderella who was safe now forever with her Prince.

Everyone rejoiced at the wedding of Cinderella to the Prince and it was blessed by all the fairies in the land.

Among the guests were the animal friends of Cinderella, who had come to help her when she needed them most. And, of course, the Fairy Rowena had a place of honour, for it was she who had made both their dreams come true.

JACK and the BEANSTALK

At the edge of a green forest stood a little cottage, whitewashed and neat, with roses making a carpet of petals in its front garden and green vines creeping round its door. Behind the cottage was a small field, where an attempt had been made to nourish the poor soil to yield a crop of potatoes and some root vegetables. A small section of the field was fenced off to provide meagre grazing for an old cow who nosed among the rocks trying to secure some nourishment for herself.

The cottage was the home of a poor boy named Jack, who lived there with his widowed mother.

On the day that our story begins, Jack's mother was worried.

"There is not a single potato, nor a turnip, nor even a carrot left to dig up," she told Jack, as she looked out the window at the rocky plot of land. "Poor Bluebell is the only thing of value we possess in the world, and now she has little enough grass left to eat."

"I will take her through the wood tomorrow," promised Jack. "I know where there are some grassy patches she can feed on."

"I'm sorry, Jack," replied his mother, "I know that Bluebell is the only companion you have. But this time she must go, otherwise we'll both starve. You must take her to market tomorrow and sell her for the best price you can."

The market was a long way off, through the woods and along the winding road round the big lake. So Jack decided to set out very early in the morning.

The sun was just peeping up from behind the hill, turning the dewdrops on the leaves into glistening diamonds, as Jack tied a rope around Bluebell's neck.

He put his cheek affectionately for a moment against the animal's lean side.

" Never fear, old friend, I'll find you a good, kind master. We have a long journey before us, but I've gathered some leaves to refresh you on the way."

Quickly at first, and then more and more slowly, they walked through the deep shadows of the tall trees.

As they walked along through the silent forest there was only the noise of Bluebell's deep breathing and the soft crunching of dried leaves under them.

Then Jack suddenly halted, pulling Bluebell's rope gently. He was certain he had heard somebody singing.

Yes! There it was again, a funny, piping little voice singing a song he had never heard before, and it came from the other side of that big oak tree.

Quiet as a mouse, Jack peeped cautiously round the tree, but his astonishment was greater than his caution and he could not help letting out a little gasp at the sight that met his eyes.

Sitting cross-legged against the tree trunk was a little man dressed all in green, an old man with silvery white hair hanging down to his shoulders.

Gathered in a circle around him, and obviously enjoying the gay little song he was singing to them, were a dog, a cat, a goat and a black foal.

He stopped singing abruptly when he saw Jack, although he paid no attention to the boy but went immediately to Bluebell.

"That's a beautiful cow you have, son," he said. "But why are you walking her through the forest? Don't you know cows prefer to sit in a field, chewing grass and counting butterflies as they pass by?"

"I am taking Bluebell to market to sell her," said Jack. And he explained to the little man why his mother had decided they must sell the cow.

"Let me buy Bluebell from you," said the man in green. "I have no cow among my friends and I would be very pleased to look after her. I have no money, but in exchange for Bluebell I will give you these magic beans."

He opened his hand to let Jack see six bright green beans lying there.

"Bluebell *would* be happy with you, I know," said Jack, so he took the magic beans and turned back home.

" What am I to do with such a stupid boy as you," said his mother, when Jack told her the story. " Do you think these beans will provide us with even one supper? We will starve now for sure, for we have nothing else that we can sell."

And, taking the hard beans from Jack, she threw them out of the window in anger.

Jack didn't trouble to go out and look for them. He didn't suppose they were any use anyway. He hadn't believed the little green man when he told him they were magic beans. Indeed he knew he'd acted foolishly giving Bluebell to him, but the queer little man loved animals so much that Jack knew Bluebell would have a good home with him.

Both Jack and his mother were hungry that night and, to avoid his mother's looks of disappointment, Jack went to bed very early.

The next morning, when Jack woke up he thought he was lying in among the centre branches of a leafy tree, for his room was dim and filled with a greenish light. The sun was not streaming in the window as it usually did, indeed the window itself looked green.

Jack jumped quickly out of bed, pushed open the window and leaned out.

Then he saw that the beans his mother had thrown out of the window the previous night had grown into a giant beanstalk. Its leaves were deep and glossy and its stalk as thick as the trunk of a mighty oak. And it grew up and up and up, out of sight into the sky.

" Whatever can be at the top of the beanstalk?" Jack said to his mother, but the poor, bewildered woman was frightened of the enchanted thing and she tried to persuade her adventurous son not to go near it.

" But the little green man was kind," said Jack. " I know he wouldn't have meant the magic beans to harm me. Don't worry, mother, I'll soon be back, but I must see what's at the top of that beanstalk."

Up and up and up Jack climbed. The sun grew hotter and hotter on his bare head and he became dizzy as he looked down on the little patchwork of fields and roads and forests that lay far beneath him.

Then, suddenly, there were only clouds below him, great puffy clouds lit up in places by the sunlight slanting through them.

Jack stepped off the beanstalk onto grass which was greener than any grass he had ever seen before. All around grew the most wonderful plants and trees and, in the silvery light that lit up this strange land, he could see, in the distance, a castle which glittered and sparkled like a jewel.

Fascinated, Jack began to walk towards the marvellous castle. But, as he drew near, a little old lady seemed to spring up out of nowhere before him.

"Do not enter the castle of the giant," she warned Jack. "For everyone on this beautiful land is his prisoner and he will make you his slave, too, if he can catch you."

"I'm not afraid," Jack replied. "I have nothing to lose except my life, and I will starve to death anyway if I stay at home."

The castle door was open, so Jack walked right in.

97

Through another door he went and into a magnificent room, richly furnished and comfortable.

But just then he heard a noise like thunder. As he listened it grew louder and louder.

Somebody was coming into the room . . . but who could make such a noise?

Crouching under a table Jack saw the largest pair of boots he had ever seen, striding towards him. He looked up and up and up, until he came to the giant's large red face with its shaggy black beard.

" *Fee, fi, fo, fum,*
I smell the blood of an Englishman.
Be he alive or be he dead,
I'll grind his bones to make my bread."

Jack shivered as the giant's bloodthirsty roar echoed through the big room. But the boy hid behind a table-leg when the giant stooped down to look for him.

Then, as a dozen slaves carried in trays piled high with food, the giant settled down to eat his midday meal.

He ate six whole chickens, a dozen roasts of beef, dishfuls of peas and carrots and enough potatoes to feed an army. And for dessert he had a cherry tart as big as a wash tub.

Jack could hardly believe it. The giant, in one meal, had eaten as much food as would do Jack and his mother for a month or more.

At last the giant finished.

" Bring me my gold," he roared, and six servants brought in six bags full of gold pieces.

Counting his money the giant fell fast asleep, snoring loudly as he sprawled across the table.

Then Jack climbed boldly up the leg of the table. He crawled over the giant's fuzzy beard, seized a bag of gold pieces and slid down the other side of the table.

The giant was so full of food that he never even woke up !

Jack's mother cried with joy as he emptied the bag of gold pieces onto their kitchen table.

"We have enough gold here to live comfortably for the rest of our lives," she said. "We will buy another cow, some chickens and ducks. And I will make new curtains for the windows and new clothes for both of us."

She was frightened when Jack planned to go up the beanstalk again the next day. But the boy was determined.

"All the people living in that beautiful land would be happy were it not for the giant," Jack said. "He is very wicked and he must be punished."

So the next morning Jack climbed up the bean-stalk again. He entered the castle through the open door and hid under the big table to await the giant's coming.

It was not long before he heard the loud thump of the giant's footsteps and heard his roar:

" *Fee, fi, fo, fum,*
I smell the blood of an Englishman.
Be he alive or be he dead,
I'll grind his bones to make my bread."

This time the giant ate a whole lamb, with potatoes and vegetables by the ton and followed it with a cheese the size of a barrel.

Afterwards, at his command, a servant brought a live white hen which he placed on the table before the giant.

"Lay, hen, lay!" roared the giant and, to Jack's astonishment, the hen laid a golden egg.

Jack could hardly wait until the giant fell asleep to seize the white hen and carry it home with him, down the beanstalk.

The next morning, despite his mother's fearful protests, Jack climbed the beanstalk again.

Again he entered the castle through the open door and again he hid under the table to await the giant. And again the giant roared:

> " *Fee, fi, fo, fum,*
> *I smell the blood of an Englishman.*
> *Be he alive or be he dead,*
> *I'll grind his bones to make my bread.*"

This time the giant was in a very angry mood.

As he searched round the room he was shouting all the while:

> " *Somebody bold*
> *stole my gold;*
> *and it must be human men*
> *who stole my magic hen.*"

He looked under the cushions on the huge armchairs, behind the books on the shelves.

"I know I smell boy," he bellowed, and he lifted the tablecloth to look under the table.

He would probably have found Jack this time, had not his dinner arrived just at that moment.

102

Fifty sausages with six great dishfuls of beans and ten plates piled high with potatoes kept the giant going only a short while.

"More food!" he roared. "I'm hungry still."

So twelve men carried in a rice pudding as big as a swimming pool.

This satisfied the giant and, the meal over, he called for his magic harp.

A golden harp was placed before him on the table and, at the giant's command, it played music so sweet that even the song of the birds seemed dull in comparison.

"That music would make my mother very happy," thought Jack, and he waited impatiently for the soothing music to lull the giant to sleep.

At last he heard the loud snores of the sleeping giant and, clambering up, he seized the golden harp and made off with it.

But, as he was sliding down the table leg, his toe caught in one of the harp strings.

Ping! Immediately the harp commenced to play. The music was entrancingly sweet but Jack, running for his life, was in no mood to be enchanted by sweet sounds.

As he ran across the floor and out through the door he pulled and tugged at the strings in an attempt to quieten them, but all in vain.

As the notes rang out the giant woke and, as Jack slipped and slithered down the front steps of the castle, he could hear the giant's footsteps pounding after him.

Closer and closer the giant drew until, still clutching the singing harp, Jack swung himself onto the beanstalk.

Jack, who was small and light, slid down the beanstalk easily. But it was more difficult for the giant. The stalk quivered and shook under his massive weight, and even more violently at the sound of his voice.

" *Fee, fi, fo, fum,*
This time I'll catch the clever one,
Who stole my harp, my gold, my hen,
I'll make him do the work of ten."

" Quick, mother," shouted Jack, as he neared the bottom of the beanstalk. " Bring me the big axe."

On reaching the ground, Jack seized the axe and hacked at the tough beanstalk. At last, with a great crash, it fell to the ground, catapulting the giant away across the tall trees, over the lake, so that he was never seen or heard of ever again.

Jack and his mother lived happily for many years. The little cottage shone with new paint now; there were flowers in the garden and animals on the farm. And there was always plenty for everyone to eat.

The giant's gold lasted Jack and his mother for a long time and, even when it had all gone, whenever they were short of money the magic hen would lay them as many golden eggs as they wanted.

GOLDILOCKS
AND THE THREE BEARS

IN the middle of a green forest lived three brown bears: Papa Bear, Mamma Bear and a baby bear called Bruno.

They were a happy family . . . at least Bruno was happy most of the time. But sometimes he felt lonely, for he had no playmates. No other bears lived in the forest, only squirrels and rabbits and birds. And even a baby bear was much too big and rough to play with such small creatures.

"I wish I could play with my new ball," Bruno said sadly one morning.

"Papa and I will play with you," his mother promised, and she woke Papa Bear who was still snoring loudly.

"Yes, yes," he said, in his big gruff voice. "We will go before breakfast while the day is cool."

So off the bear family went, into the woods.

Along another path through the trees a little girl wandered, picking wildflowers. Her name was Priscilla, but everyone called her Goldilocks because her hair was golden as wheat, bright as a shining new penny.

She had come a long way, for the flowers were so pretty that she kept following them on and on. Each time she picked one she saw a nicer one just a little way ahead.

Until, suddenly, she came out of the tall dark trees into the bright sunlight. There was a great silence here. The singing of the birds had followed her among the trees, but here there were no trees and no birds, not even the rustle of leaves. Everything was very still and, for a moment, Goldilocks felt frightened.

Then, just in front of her, she saw the dearest little house. It had a gay tiled roof, like a patchwork quilt; latticed windows with shining panes and bright green shutters, and a vivid pink door.

Goldilocks knocked at the door.

Rat-a-tat-tat! the sound rang out in the quiet clearing.

But nobody answered.

Rat-a-tat-tat! she knocked louder this time.

But again there was no reply.

All was silent inside the little house.

Disappointed, Goldilocks was about to turn away when she noticed that there was no lock on the door. She turned the handle and the door swung inwards with a faint creak.

Timidly, Goldilocks peeped round the door.

"Is anybody home?" she called.

She waited for an answer, but there was no sound except the crackle of the log fire.

"Can I come in, please?" she called, a little louder.

But nobody answered.

Now she knew that it was wrong to go into the house when nobody was at home. But it was such a dear little house and she was a very curious little girl. So . . . .

She tiptoed in and looked about her. The first thing she saw was a big oblong table. It was laid for breakfast, with a bright checked cloth and a vase of pretty flowers. On the table also were three bowls of porridge, with steam still rising from it. Suddenly Goldilocks began to feel very hungry.

She took a spoonful of porridge from the great, big, enormous, blue bowl. Ugh! somebody had put salt on it and it tasted just horrid.

Next she sampled a spoonful from the middle-sized, red bowl. Ugh! that was like syrup, sickly sweet.

Well, there was still another bowl of porridge. Goldilocks took a spoonful from the little, wee, tiny, green bowl. She smiled happily, for it was delicious. Not salty, yet not too sweet . . . in fact, just the way she liked it.

And, as she felt hungry, she ate it all up.

Her hunger satisfied, Goldilocks wandered round the little room. The house was just as nice inside as it had looked from the outside. The room was dotted with vases and bowls of flowers. Pretty curtains hung on all the windows and a lovely smell of pine trees filled the air from the burning logs.

In front of the blazing fire were three armchairs. It looked so cosy and comfortable, and all of a sudden Goldilocks began to feel tired after her long walk.

But which chair should she sit in?

One, two, three.

One of them must surely be just the right size for her.

There was a great, big, enormous chair, with padded back and purple cushions. Goldilocks climbed into it and sat down. But she only filled a little corner of the seat and her legs stuck out straight in a most uncomfortable way. She climbed down carefully and went to the next chair.

This was a middle-sized rocking chair. It was great fun at first, like riding a horse. But as the chair was still too big she kept sliding from side to side as the chair went back and forth. Soon she began to feel like a little boat, tossed about on a rough sea. She climbed down very quickly from the middle-sized chair.

The third chair was a little, wee, tiny, wooden chair. It was really very small. Goldilocks squeezed and squeezed to fit herself in. At last she plopped down heavily.

Crash! The little, wee, tiny chair broke into pieces, tumbling Goldilocks on the floor.

She wasn't hurt at all but oh! that dear little chair! Not all the king's horses nor all the king's men would ever put it together again.

She looked around guiltily, but nobody was there to see.

Goldilocks decided to explore further.

In one corner of the room was a wooden staircase. The little girl climbed up carefully, step by step. It opened straight into a bedroom, with three beds standing side by side along one wall.

There was a great, big, enormous bed of dark oak with a bright green bedspread. As Goldilocks was still tired she slipped off her shoes and climbed up on this bed. But it was hard and knobbly.

She decided to try the second bed.

This was a medium-sized bed, painted green and with a dark red cover. When Goldilocks lay down in this bed it was so soft that it seemed to swallow her up. Every place she moved became a deep feathery hole and she had to burrow herself out like a little mole to reach the edge of the bed.

She slipped on to the floor and looked at the third bed.

It was a little, wee, tiny bed of pale blue with flowers painted on it and a pretty blue flowery bedspread. Beside it stood a bookcase filled with story books and on the other side was a shelf with a large waxy candle in a holder. On the wall behind the bed hung a picture of a baby bear.

"Why that must be the little boy's favourite toy," thought Goldilocks, for of course she did not know that this was the house of the three bears.

She put her shoes neatly on the floor and hung up her pretty straw hat before she climbed on to the bed. It was neither too hard nor too soft.

In fact it was so comfortable that she put her head down on the white frilly pillow and fell fast asleep.

At this moment the bears returned from the forest, with Bruno running ahead. He had enjoyed his game though, of course, he had won easily, because Papa was too stiff and Mamma too fat to run very fast.

Bruno reached the house first.

"Mamma, Papa," he called in his tiny little voice, "the door is wide open!"

"You must be more careful, my dear," boomed Papa to his wife, "for of course it must have been you who left the door open."

With Mamma protesting, in her high squeaky voice, that she had never done this, they went into the house.

Mamma rushed over to the table to see that everything was ready for their breakfast. Then she noticed something odd.

"Papa! Papa!" she called excitedly. "Come here and see. Come quickly!"

Papa came. And he looked. Everything seemed all right to him. He wished Mamma would stop fussing and get his breakfast. He was very hungry after all that exercise.

"But the spoons," Mamma said. "I left three spoons on the table and now they are each sitting in a bowl."

Papa Bear lifted his spoon out of his great, big, enormous bowl. It was all sticky.

"Bears o' bears," his voice was like a thunderclap. "Somebody's been eating my porridge."

"Oh dear! Oh dear!" squeaked Mamma Bear. "Somebody's been eating my porridge too."

And then Bruno went to his dish. He lifted up the spoon but there was nothing under it. His dish was quite empty.

"Somebody's been eating my porridge and eaten it all up," he wailed. "And I'm such a hungry little bear too."

Papa Bear was angry.

"We must search the house," he growled.

As he turned from the table he saw his big comfortable armchair. But the newspapers he had placed neatly on it were now scattered on the floor.

"Ho ho! Ho hum! Somebody's been sitting in my chair," he said.

Mamma rushed round picking up the newspapers. Then she noticed the ball of wool lying on the floor. She knew she had left it on her chair beside the jumper she was knitting for Bruno.

"Me too! Me too!" she shrilled. "Somebody's been sitting in my chair."

Hearing a little sob they both turned to see big tears running down Bruno's furry cheeks.

"Boo-hoo-hoo!" he cried. "Somebody's been sitting in my chair and they've, boo-hoo, broken it all up!"

But Mamma gave him a big bear hug and Papa promised to make him a new chair the very next day, so he soon stopped crying.

"We must find the stranger in our house," growled Papa. "Let us look upstairs."

Bruno went first, because he liked to run up stairs. But Papa's legs were very stiff and Mamma was very fat, so they puffed and panted up behind him.

In the bedroom, Papa walked over to his big black bed. He knew that Mamma had straightened the green bedspread that morning, but now it was tossed and tumbled.

"Somebody's been lying in my bed," he rumbled, and his voice shook the pictures on the wall.

"And somebody's been lying in my bed," squeaked Mamma.

Bruno danced with excitement.

"Mamma! Papa! Come here! Come here! For somebody's been lying in my bed and she's still in it."

Just then Goldilocks, disturbed by the noise, awoke.

She saw the big bear with his green striped trousers, a gold watch-chain hanging from his red waistcoat and his smart bow tie. Then she looked at the middle-sized bear in her flowery hat and with a white frilly apron over her blue dress. And, last of all, she saw Bruno. She was certain it was only a dream until. . . .

"Bears o' bears, and who are you?" boomed Papa in his big hoarse voice.

There were no voices as loud as that in a dream.

Goldilocks jumped up and, gathering up her shoes and hat, she dashed past the three bears. Down the stairs she fled, through the open door and over the grass towards the forest.

Even Bruno could not catch her.

As she reached the woods she looked back. The bears looked friendly really, perhaps they would not have harmed her. But she was not sure, you see she had never met a bear family before.

Perhaps one day her mummy will take her back to the bears' house. Then Goldilocks and Bruno could play with the green ball. They might even play hide-and-seek together among the tall green trees.

NURSERY RHYMES

THERE WAS AN OLD WOMAN

There was an old woman who lived in a shoe,
She had so many children, she didn't know what to do.
She gave them some broth, without any bread,
Then whipped them all souhdly and sent them to bed.

PRAYER

There are four corners on my bed.
There are four angels at its head.
Matthew, Mark, Luke and John,
Bless the bed that I lie on.

TWINKLE, TWINKLE

Twinkle, twinkle, little star,
How I wonder what you are!
Up above the world so high,
Like a diamond in the sky.

TOM THUMB

MANY. many years ago, England was ruled by a great king whose name was Arthur. He was a wise and a just king and all the country prospered under his rule.

To the court of King Arthur came the greatest musicians and the cleverest scholars, the bravest knights and the wisest counsellors. And, especially near and dear to the king, there was a magician of marvellous powers called Merlin.

But Merlin did not remain close to Arthur all the time. For this man of magic knew that the power of kings came not from their courtiers but from the common people who had never been inside the palace gates. If he would continue to be great, Arthur must know the hopes and the fears of all his subjects. And so that he might keep his king well informed, Merlin, disguised as a poor traveller, would wander round the country-side talking to the people and living in their homes.

So it was that one day he visited the home of a humble peasant and his wife. Taking him to be a poor beggar, they shared their humble meal with him willingly.

They were good people, thought Merlin, as he talked with them. He admired the well-scrubbed neatness of their home and the well-tended orderliness of their small farm. Yet, even while they smiled, he sensed their deep sadness. This was not good; all the subjects of King Arthur should be happy and content.

"You have a good life together," Merlin addressed the couple. "Your home is comfortable, you have enough to eat and few worries. Why, then, are you both so unhappy?"

"Oh, indeed, we have a lot to be thankful for, and a lot more than most people," said the farmer's wife. "But the years go by and still we have no children. If only we had a child no bigger than my thumb we would be the happiest couple in the land."

No bigger than my thumb . . . the idea amused the mighty Merlin. Could it be done, he wondered . . .

"I can see no reason why you shouldn't have your wish," he laughed, and he walked out of the house, leaving the poor couple staring in amazement after him.

Later, by the power of the great Merlin, the couple did have a child, a little boy who was perfect in every way and as bright and intelligent as any parents could wish . . . but he was no more than two inches high. So they christened him Tom Thumb.

The tiny fellow was a great joy to his parents whose only problem now was how to clothe him, for human hands could not sew such tiny clothes as he would need.

Their problem came to the ears of the queen of the fairies. Curious to see the little boy, she visited the farm the next day.

"You should be very happy to have such a beautiful little boy," she told Tom's parents. "And I shall be delighted to have my own tailors make him the finest clothes."

An oak leaf had he for his crown;
His shirt of web by spiders spun;
With jackets wove of thistledown,
His trousers were of feathers done.
His stockings of apple rind they tie
With eyelash from his mother's eye;
His shoes were made of mouse's skin,
Tanned with the downy hair within.

Tom Thumb was very proud of his splendid costume, nor did his lack of size daunt him; he strutted round the countryside like a giant.

He was a lively boy, always merry and full of pranks. And, despite his small size, he was often useful to his father on the farm.

There was a day when his father decided to clear some woodland.

" I wish there was someone who could bring the cart through the woods for me," he remarked to his wife.

" Let me do it," piped up Tom Thumb.

" Why, a little fellow like you couldn't drive the cat, let alone the big farm horse," laughed his mother.

" Just put me into the horse's ear and I promise I'll take him straight to my father," said Tom, when the time had come for his father to want the cart.

His mother did as he asked, more to amuse the boy than because she believed he could do as he said.

But clever Tom whispered into the old horses' ear, guiding him safely through the woods.

Tom's spirit of adventure often got him into trouble. There was the time when he dived into the goldfish bowl for a swim and was chased around by the fish for hours before his mother fished him out.

Then the big tortoise-shell cat almost mistook him for a mouse as he emerged from his exploration of the mousehole which she'd been watching all morning.

Another day, while he was playing in the long grass, he was almost swallowed by the black and white cow. But she quickly spat him out again when Tom battered sharply with his little fists on her tongue.

Nor was that the end of Tom's adventures

One day Tom's mother was making a cake. Tom, ever curious, climbed up on the edge of the bowl when his mother wasn't looking. Standing on the edge, he leaned too far out and lost his balance. Down he fell into the mixture.

He tried to call out, but the batter got in his mouth and he couldn't say a word. He was baking in the oven before he could utter a word. For the first time in his life he felt frightened. He banged on the sides of the tin and jumped around.

The noise of the tin jumping about in the oven frightened his mother.

"This cake must be bewitched," thought the poor woman. And she threw it out of the window.

It landed in some bushes where a tinker found it later. He put it in his bag, intending to eat it for his supper.

But when he started to eat it he got quite a shock.

"Put me down! Put me down!" came a little voice.

Terrified, the poor man threw the cake down and ran for his life.

Just then a raven, flying overhead, saw something squirming on the ground. Thinking it might be a delicate morsel and feeling a bit peckish at the time, the raven picked Tom up in his beak. But, accustomed as he was to wriggly worms, the raven found Tom a much more troublesome mouthful. For Tom danced on the bird's tongue and punched his jaws. After a short struggle, the raven dropped Tom out of his beak, right in the middle of the sea.

Tom shot down through the clear blue water. Then, suddenly, darkness surrounded the boy. He guessed, and rightly, that he had been swallowed by a fish. But he was so seasick he lost all count of time.

The fish was soon caught and brought to the kitchen of the palace. So the next thing Tom knew the fish was slit open and, glad to be on dry land again, Tom climbed out . . . right in the middle of King Arthur's table.

How the King and his Knights laughed at the sight of the tiny boy standing on the edge of the big serving dish!

King Arthur was charmed by the gay little fellow, who also became a great favorite with all the knights and ladies of the court.

He was treated like a prince of the realm. A tiny golden castle was built for him in the king's gardens, complete with towers and moat, and he had his own golden chair in Arthur's throne room. When the king went riding Tom often sat in front of him on his great white charger, and the king had a specially made silk pouch hung on his belt so that Tom might rest in it when he felt weary.

Tom Thumb repaid all this kindness by bringing laughter and happiness into the sober life of the court. He was always up to some merry prank: hiding in somebody's pocket so that he might pinch and tease them, causing them to laugh most heartily when they should be most solemn; perching on the king's drinking goblet like a giant bee or, when he dared, coasting down Merlin's long white beard.

Now, in those days, great tournaments were held, in which the knights opposed each other on horseback, fighting with swords till one of them was thrown off his horse. Tom longed to join in this sport, so the fairies were called in consultation to see how this might be arranged.

After much discussion, it was decided that a white mouse should be trained to be Tom's faithful steed. The mouse was fitted with a bridle and saddle of the softest red leather. Tom himself was clad in a silver coat of armour. His sword was a darning needle fitted into a handle which was encrusted with tiny gems.

Now the little fellow could accompany the court on his own mount as they rode to hunt. So brave was he that, to the delight of the king, he even engaged in battle with opponents much bigger than himself, and he became the toast of the tournaments for his courage, and sometimes even for his victory.

But, as might be expected, some of the courtiers became jealous of the delight which Arthur took in his tiniest knight. And they plotted among themselves how they might bring him to disgrace.

Hearing their evil rumours and fearing that the king might believe them, Tom crawled into an empty snail shell one day and hid there until he was almost starved to death.

But as he lay there, hungry and dispirited, the intelligent little fellow thought about his problem and decided that this was indeed a foolish way to try to solve it. He must leave the king's court altogether; somewhere, in the kingdom, he would find a place to hide where he could live a simple life in safety.

So, venturing out, he spied a bright-winged butterfly. This would carry him at least part of the long journey, Tom thought, so he hopped on to the butterfly's back.

But the palace gardens were full of beautiful flowers and the butterfly was quite content to remain within the walls, flitting from flower to fragrant flower.

It so happened that, on this morning, King Arthur was taking a walk through his rose gardens when he spied the bright butterfly with its tiny passenger. He had been very concerned about Tom's disappearance and now, unless he caught him, the little fellow might be lost to him forever.

Immediately he began to chase the butterfly and soon the whole court joined in the pursuit.

Through the rose beds and the beautifully tended flower borders they scrambled; up and down the fruit trees; through the strawberry beds and over the wall where the vines climbed. The gardeners looked on in dismay and then they, too, dropped their tools to join in the chase.

The butterfly began to resent all this unwelcome attention, and at last he turned upside down in the air so that his little passenger was thrown off his back.

Down Tom fell, through the air and into the big watering can that one of the gardeners had just dropped. He would have surely drowned had not one of the pages seen him fall. He fished Tom out, dripping and gasping.

King Arthur and his court welcomed the tiny knight back with much joy and celebration, and even those who had been jealous of him before were glad to have him back again. He went back to live in his tiny golden castle, and his parents were given a house nearby.

From that day forth none dared harm Tom Thumb. By King Arthur's order, great Merlin protected the tiny person with his mighty powers. So Tom lived on, the smallest, but by no means the least famous, of King Arthur's court.

LITTLE
Red Riding Hood

"HURRY up, Jane! It is just one o'clock. If you set out now you will be home again before darkness falls." So saying, the mother hurried to pack the basket which the little girl had to take to her sick grandmother, who lived on the other side of the woods.

She put in all sorts of delicious and nourishing things to eat: honey and cheese, home-made jam and buns, and a large iced chocolate cake. She covered the basket with a blue-checked cloth.

Jane put on her favourite red cloak, which tied under her chin with a matching ribbon and had a hood to protect her from the cold winds. But as this was a sunny Spring day she left her bright hair uncovered.

"Now come back quickly, Jane. And remember that you must speak to no strangers on the way," her mother warned her.

"Dont worry, mummy, I'll be all right."

Jane waved goodbye as she started her journey through the forest.

She felt happy and excited. This was a great adventure, the first time she had been allowed through the woods by herself.

But she knew the way very well. For every week she and her mummy went to visit her grandmother.

She was not frightened at all, for what was there to fear? It was not really dark among the tall trees, for the sun slanted through them to make bright patterns on the grass. Birds left their nests to swoop down and circle her as they sang and the shy deer let her stroke them gently as she passed.

Over the twittering of the birds Jane heard a loud noise which was repeated again and again, becoming louder and louder. It was almost like the footsteps of a giant tramping through the forest, she thought. And she felt frightened.

But, as she turned a bend in the path, she saw a woodman plying his axe as he cut a stout tree trunk into neat logs. How silly she was! A giant, indeed! Her mother had told her that there were no giants any more.

"Hello, Red Riding Hood,"

the woodman greeted her, for her fondness for her red cloak had earned her this nickname. "What are you doing in the woods all by yourself?"

"My grandmother is ill," Jane replied "and I am taking her some food to nourish her and make her well again."

Concealed behind a near-by tree Willy Wolf listened, and he licked his lips greedily at the thought of all that mouth-watering food. And if that did not satisfy his hunger, the little girl herself would make a tasty

mouthful. He watched her with an evil grin.

"Take care, Red Riding Hood," called the friendly woodman, and Jane waved back happily.

But Willy Wolf followed her. Darting from tree to tree, he took good care that the woodman didn't see him, for he knew that the woodman would recognise him immediately for the wicked wolf that he was.

Continuing on her way, Jane stopped farther along the path to watch the flight of a butterfly as it flitted from flower to flower.

How gay the flowers looked, bowing gracefully in the breeze. And what lovely colours: pale yellow, deep blue, pink, and snow-white with a bright yellow eye. She must pick some for Granny, who loved pretty things.

Sitting on a log, Willy Wolf watched irritably.

He knew that he dare not pounce on the little girl here, because the woodman would surely hear her screams and rush to her rescue with his sharp axe. Willy Wolf shivered at the awful thought.

On the other hand he was very hungry indeed and he became even more bad-tempered and impatient than usual when it was past his mealtime.

So he fumed and fretted as Jane chose her flowers carefully. Dare he snatch her basket? At the thought of all the goodies it contained his long tongue hung out eagerly and his coat bristled with impatience.

Unable to keep still, he paced back and forth, to and fro, up and down.

Suddenly Jane looked up and saw him. She stared at him curiously. She was sure she had never seen *him* in the woods before. He was so queer, with his funny sticking-up ears, that she knew she would have remembered him. But perhaps it wasn't his fault that his ears had grown so long, she thought, for she was a kind-hearted little girl.

So she didn't run away but stood still, smiling at the wolf.

Willy Wolf walked up to her.

"Where are you going, little girl?" he asked, softening his hoarse voice so as not to frighten her.

Jane remembered her mother's warning about speaking to strangers. But although he looked odd, he certainly didn't look dangerous, she decided. So she answered him politely.

"Well I should hurry along then, if I were you," said Willy Wolf, thinking of his overdue meal.

But as Jane followed the path, Willy Wolf took a shorter route through the trees so that he reached the grandmother's cottage first.

The door was open, for the old lady had been expecting her grandchild.

Quickly and quietly he entered the house and then tiptoed into the bedroom. Taken by surprise, Jane's grandmother was soon overcome by the wolf, who bundled her into the wardrobe. For although he was very hungry, he had a tastier morsel in mind. He licked his lips at the thought of the little girl in the red cloak and her basket full of goodies.

But he must be very quick, for the little girl would even now be approaching the house.

He searched through the drawers, full of neatly folded clothes, until he found one of Granny's large white nightgowns. He pulled it on hastily over his own clothes. Then he found a lace bedcap, which tied under his chin with pink ribbons. He clambered into bed, boots and all.

He was just in time, for he could hear a gentle tapping on the door.

"Can I come in Granny?

He heard the little girl call.

"I have brought you a basket full of good things to eat to make you well again."

"Come in, come in, my dear," he called, making his voice sound soft and weak. "Turn the handle and the door will open."

He heard Jane coming in. Then the door closed gently behind her.

"I've been expecting you," he murmured, as he grinned evilly to himself.

Jane entered the living-room, where she noticed that Granny had set the table for their tea. Without waiting to take off her cloak she went over to the bedroom door, knocked, and waited.

"Enter, Little Red Riding Hood. I've been waiting such a long time for you."

Jane was surprised. This was the first time Granny had ever called her by this nickname.

Sudenly the house seemed very quiet.

There was just the noise of the big clock.

Tick! Tock! Tick! Tock!

Jane felt just a little bit frightened.

For a moment she felt like running back home through the woods to her mummy.

But she pushed open the door and walked into the bedroom.

Her fears vanished.

How silly she had been!

At the far end of the room was her grandmother's big bed, with its frilly white pillows and its gay flowered bedspread. Beside it, on a little table, were the pills and medicines which the doctor had given her to make her well again.

Although it was such a warm day Jane noticed that Granny kept the bedclothes pulled right up to her chin. As she wore a lacey bedcap there was very little of her face to be seen.

"Come over here, child," came a voice from the bed as Jane stood by the door.

But as she went closer Jane felt puzzled.

"Why Granny, what big, big eyes you've got," said the little girl.

"All the better to see you, my dear."

Jane went closer.

"And your ears. How very long they've grown," said Jane.

"All the better to hear you, my dear."

Now Jane was standing right beside the bed.

"But your teeth, Granny. They're so long and sharp, just like a . . ."

But Willy Wolf could wait no longer for his meal.

"Yes, my teeth are long and very sharp. Just right, in fact, for eating up sweet little girls like you!"

In the wardrobe poor Granny pushed and pulled, trying in vain to force open the locked door so that she might save her dear grandchild from the wicked wolf.

Poor Jane was unable to move with fright. She watched as the wolf thrust one booted foot, and then the second one, out of the bed.

She knew she should try to escape, but her legs just refused to move. She stood quite still as he came towards her. But, at last, the sight of his big sharp teeth and his long tongue hanging out roused her and she screamed with all her might.

Scream after scream rang out through the quiet house and echoed in the woods, so that even Willy Wolf felt like covering up his ears.

A short distance away Jane's friend the woodman was sitting down to eat his sandwiches when he heard the frightened call.

"Help! Help!"

In great haste he picked up his axe and started off in the direction of the cottage, covering the ground rapidly with his long strides.

As he neared the house the screams grew louder and the woodman hurried even faster.

By the time he reached the house Jane was running wildly through the rooms, in and out of the doors and round the furniture, followed closely by Willy Wolf.

Truth to tell Willy Wolf was not feeling very happy at all. He had never imagined that such a little girl could make such a loud noise and it was beginning to give him a big headache.

But both his headache and his hunger were forgotten when he saw the woodman enter the room, his shining axe on his shoulder.

With no hesitation at all Willy Wolf jumped out of the window and dashed for the shelter of the trees.

How he wished he had been a wiser wolf and left the little girl to pick her silly flowers! He would surely have had indigestion anyway after such a noisy meal! He resolved that as long as he lived he would never again wish for a human for his dinner. A nice fat rabbit or even a hare was much more to his liking anyway.

He ran on and on and on. At first he kept tripping over Granny's nightgown and falling headlong. So, as he ran, he ripped off the nightgown so that he might travel faster. But the bedcap still remained on his head, its ribbons flying out behind him.

Soon darkness came and the moon peeped out shyly. But still Willy Wolf ran on. He was so frightened of that big gleaming axe that he never once slowed down to find out if the woodman was still following him.

He really was a funny sight: a frightened wolf in a lacey cap. All the animals of the forest came out to laugh at him, for the tale of the frightened wolf was carried by the birds right through the forest. Poor Willy Wolf! You couldn't help feeling just a little bit sorry for him, now that he had learned his lesson.

Meanwhile, back at the cottage the woodman had released Jane's grandmother from the wardrobe in which Willy Wolf had locked her.

She was so happy and relieved that Jane was safe that she did not feel ill any more.

"How can we ever thank you?" she asked the woodman.

I am very happy that I was at hand," the woodman replied, "for we are all very fond of our Little Red Riding Hood."

"You must stay and have tea with us." Granny unpacked all the dainty things which Jane's mother had sent. "And whenever you are in this part of the woods you must always come in and let me give you a meal."

The woodman replied that he would be very happy indeed to do this.

So, as Willy Wolf ran on wearily, the noise of happy laughter rang out from the cottage at the edge of the forest.